Happy Valentine's Day to:

_____

Click, Clack, Moo
I LOVE YOU!

Doreen Cronin · *Illustrated by* **Betsy Lewin**

A CAITLYN DLOUHY BOOK

Atheneum Books for Young Readers

New York London Toronto Sydney New Delhi

It is Valentine's Day on the farm,

but there is work to be done before the big dance.

To keep the pigs healthy,
Farmer Brown cleans the pigpen.

To keep the donkey happy,
Farmer Brown stocks the stable.

To keep the animals safe
from foxes and raccoons,
Farmer Brown mends
the fence.

Little Duck worked hard, too.
She tied balloons to…everything.
She hung streamers from…everything.

She strung sparkling lights
between…everything.

She made hearts out of anything she could find.

When Little Duck was finished,
there was paint on her face,
glitter in her wings,
and a valentine for everyone!

That evening,
Little Duck greeted each guest at the door.
The chickens arrived first.

Little Duck handed each chicken a valentine.
The chickens handed her a casserole.

The pigs arrived next.

quack quack quack!

Little Duck handed each pig a valentine.
The pigs handed her chips and salsa.

The sheep arrived fashionably late.
quack quack quack!
She handed each sheep a valentine.

The sheep headed right for the chips and salsa.

The cows had a more formal affair and were out for the evening.

Join us
for the second annual
DIVINE BOVINE BALL!
(Formal attire, please)

When the music came on,
the chickens danced with the chickens,

the pigs danced
with the pigs,

the sheep danced
with the sheep,

and the mice did the hustle.

On the other side of the fence,
at the top of the hill, a little fox heard the music.
She perked up her ears and called,

Yip yip yip!

Nobody answered.
But there were streamers in the trees!

Little Fox climbed down the hill.
She called,

Yip yip yip!

Nobody answered.

But there were balloons to lead the way!

Little Fox trotted down to the fence.
She called,

Yip yip yip!

Nobody answered.
But there was a trail of hearts to follow,

so Little Fox dug a hole.

Little Fox arrived at the barn,
covered in streamers and glitter.

She called,

Yip yip yip!

The chickens stopped dancing.
The sheep stopped dancing.
The pigs stopped dancing.

The mice hustled right out into the hay.

Little Fox called again,

Yip

Little Duck
was not scared.
She greeted
the new guest.

She handed Little Fox her last valentine.

Little Fox handed her a valentine right back.

Duck turned the music up.

Yip, quack, yip, quack, yip, quack quack!

The chickens
danced with
the sheep.

The pigs danced
with the chickens.

And the mice kept right on hustling.

Everybody danced with everybody until...

the
cows
came
home.

For Anna Banana, with love
—D. C.

For Ted, always
—B. L.

ATHENEUM BOOKS FOR YOUNG READERS
An imprint of Simon & Schuster Children's Publishing Division
1230 Avenue of the Americas, New York, New York 10020
Text copyright © 2017 by Doreen Cronin
Illustrations copyright © 2017 by Betsy Lewin
ATHENEUM BOOKS FOR YOUNG READERS is a registered trademark of Simon & Schuster, Inc. • Atheneum logo is a trademark of Simon & Schuster, Inc. • For information about special discounts for bulk purchases, please contact Simon & Schuster Special Sales at 1-866-506-1949 or business@simonandschuster.com. • The Simon & Schuster Speakers Bureau can bring authors to your live event. • For more information or to book an event, contact the Simon & Schuster Speakers Bureau at 1-866-248-3049 or visit our website at www.simonspeakers.com. • Book design by Ann Bobco • The text for this book was set in Filosofia. • The illustrations for this book were rendered in watercolor. • Manufactured in China • 0917 SCP • First Edition • 10 9 8 7 6 5 4 3 2 1
Library of Congress Cataloging-in-Publication Data
Names: Cronin, Doreen, author. | Lewin, Betsy, illustrator. Title: Click, clack, moo : I love you! / Doreen Cronin ; illustrated by Betsy Lewin. • Description: First edition. | New York : Atheneum Books For Young Readers, [2017] | "A Caitlyn Dlouhy Book." Summary: Little Duck is working hard making valentines for everyone and decorating for the Valentine's Day dance, but what happens when an unexpected guest arrives? • Identifiers: LCCN 2016033732 | ISBN 9781481444965 (hardcover : alk. paper) | ISBN 9781481444972 (eBook) • Subjects: | CYAC: Valentine's Day—Fiction. • Farm life—Fiction. | Ducks—Fiction. | Domestic animals—Fiction. | Dance parties—Fiction.• Classification: LCC PZ7.C88135 Cmg 2017 | DDC [EB—dc23 • LC record available at https://lccn.loc.gov/2016033732